Dear Parent:
Your child's love of reading starts here!

Every child learns to read in a different way and at his or her own speed. Some go back and forth between reading levels and read favorite books again and again. Others read through each level in order. You can help your young reader improve and become more confident by encouraging his or her own interests and abilities. From books your child reads with you to the first books he or she reads alone, there are I Can Read Books for every stage of reading:

SHARED READING
Basic language, word repetition, and whimsical illustrations, ideal for sharing with your emergent reader

BEGINNING READING
Short sentences, familiar words, and simple concepts for children eager to read on their own

READING WITH HELP
Engaging stories, longer sentences, and language play for developing readers

READING ALONE
Complex plots, challenging vocabulary, and high-interest topics for the independent reader

ADVANCED READING
Short paragraphs, chapters, and exciting themes for the perfect bridge to chapter books

I Can Read Books have introduced children to the joy of reading since 1957. Featuring award-winning authors and illustrators and a fabulous cast of beloved characters, I Can Read Books set the standard for beginning readers.

A lifetime of discovery begins with the magical words **"I Can Read!"**

Visit www.icanread.com for information
on enriching your child's reading experience.

Flat Stanley and the Haunted House. Text copyright © 2010 by the Estate of Jeff Brown. Illustrations by Macky Pamintuan, copyright © 2010 by HarperCollins Publishers. All rights reserved. Manufactured in China. No part of this book may be used or reproduced in any manner whatsoever without written permission except in the case of brief quotations embodied in critical articles and reviews. For information address HarperCollins Children's Books, a division of HarperCollins Publishers, 10 East 53rd Street, New York, NY 10022. www.icanread.com

Library of Congress catalog card number: 2009925070
ISBN 978-0-06-143004-6 (trade bdg.) — ISBN 978-0-06-143005-3 (pbk.)

10   11   12   13   14   SCP   10   9   7   6   5   4   3   2   1   ❖   First Edition

I Can Read!

READING WITH HELP 2

FLAT STANLEY
and the Haunted House

created by Jeff Brown
by Lori Haskins Houran
pictures by Macky Pamintuan

HARPER
An Imprint of HarperCollinsPublishers

Stanley Lambchop lived
with his mother, his father,
and his little brother, Arthur.

Stanley was four feet tall,

about a foot wide, and half an inch thick.

He had been flat ever since

a bulletin board fell on him.

Mostly Stanley liked being flat.

He was very good at dodgeball

and hide-and-seek.

"Will there be limbo at our party?"

asked Stanley.

He was very good at limbo, too.

"Yes," said Mrs. Lambchop.

Stanley's school was having

a Halloween party.

"I want to see the haunted house,"

said Arthur.

"I hope it's really scary!"

"Not too scary," said his mother.

"There will be small children at the party."

Mrs. Lambchop zipped up
Arthur's monster costume.
She had sewn it herself.
"Perfect," she said.
"Scary. But not too scary."

Stanley put on his costume, too.

He was a blueberry pancake.

"You look good enough to eat,"

Mrs. Lambchop said.

"Let's go!"

Arthur and Mrs. Lambchop
got in the car.
Mr. Lambchop tied Stanley
to the roof rack.
"All set, Stanley?" he asked.
"All set," Stanley answered.

The school gym was full of
pirates and witches and fairies.
"Hey, look!" Arthur said.
"Hay is for horses, Arthur,"
Mrs. Lambchop
told him.

"I know," said Arthur. "Look!"

A horse trotted by.

"Oh," said Mrs. Lambchop.

"Sorry, dear."

"There's the haunted house!"

Arthur said to Stanley.

They stood in line behind the horse.

"What a clever costume,"

the horse's mother said to Stanley.

"You look as flat as a pancake!"

At last, their turn came.

"Come on," said Stanley.

The boys stepped inside.

"BOO!" yelled a ghost.

Arthur said the ghost's sneakers

looked like Coach Bart's.

A werewolf howled.

Then it sneezed.

"Bless you!" said the ghost
politely to the werewolf.

"This isn't scary at all!" Stanley said.

"Let's get out of here, Arthur."

Outside, Arthur and Stanley

saw a little boy crying.

It was their neighbor Martin Tibbs.

"What's wrong?" asked Stanley.

"Did the haunted house scare you?"

"No." Martin sniffled.

Martin told them that a bully

had stolen his giant candy corn.

"It was my prize for winning

the limbo contest," he said sadly.

"I missed the limbo contest?

Rats!" said Stanley.

"Where did the mean kid go?"

asked Arthur.

Martin pointed across the gym.

An older boy leaned against the wall.

Next to him was the candy corn.

20

"That's one big candy corn!" said Arthur.

"That's one big kid," said Stanley.

Stanley looked at Arthur's costume.

"I have an idea," he said.

"Make room for me, Arthur!"

Stanley took off his costume

and slipped inside Arthur's.

Then he whispered in Arthur's ear.

"Great plan," Arthur said.

"Just don't blink!"

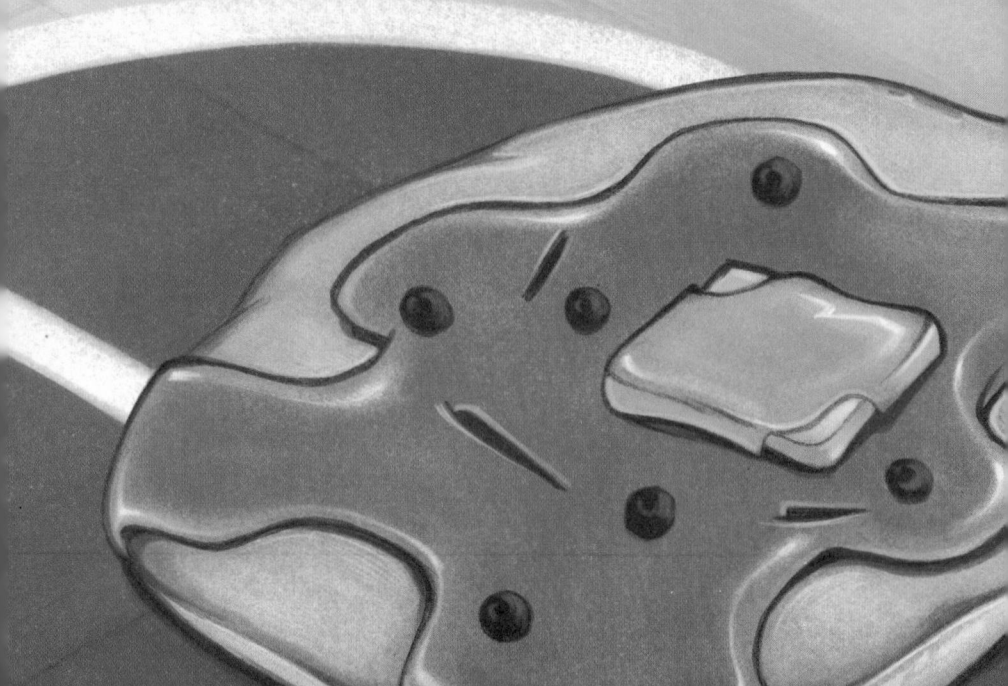

23

Arthur walked over to the big kid.

Stanley didn't blink.

"Give that candy corn back or else," Arthur demanded.

"Or else what?" said the bully.

"I'll tell everyone that you're scared of me," said Arthur.

The kid stood up tall.

He stepped right in front of Arthur and Stanley.

Stanley still didn't blink.

"Why should I be scared of you?"
the bully growled.

"I'm a two-headed monster,"
Arthur said.

The boy pointed to Stanley's face.

"Ha! That head is so fake,"
he said.

Then, Stanley blinked.

"Fake?" said Stanley. "Oh, really?"

"AAAAAAHHH!" yelled the bully.

He ran out the gym door,

leaving the candy corn behind.

"YES!" yelled Stanley and Arthur.
They jumped up and down
inside Arthur's costume.

Martin picked up his candy corn.

"Thanks, guys!"

"Uh-oh," said Arthur.

Stanley turned around.

Mr. and Mrs. Lambchop

were standing behind them.

"Arthur and Stanley Lambchop,
I saw what you did,"
Mrs. Lambchop said sternly.
"That was scary."

Then Mrs. Lambchop smiled.

"TOO scary!"